THE Charles Dickens

CHILDREN'S COLLECTION

Published by Sweet Cherry Publishing Limited
Unit 36, Vulcan House,
Vulcan Road,
Leicester, LE5 3EF
United Kingdom

First published in the US in 2021
2021 edition

2 4 6 8 10 9 7 5 3 1

ISBN: 978-1-78226-744-7

Charles Dickens: Great Expectations

Based on the original story from Charles Dickens,
adapted by Philip Gooden.

Cover design by Pipi Sposito and Margot Reverdiau
Illustrations by Pipi Sposito

Lexile® code numerical measure L = Lexile® 710L

Guided Reading Level = Q

www.sweetcherrypublishing.com

Printed and bound in India
I.TP002

Charles Dickens

GREAT EXPECTATIONS

Sweet Cherry

PIP MEETS A CONVICT

This story is about Philip Pirrip. Everyone called him Pip. He couldn't remember his mother and father because they died when he was very young.

MRS JOE

Pip's sister, who was twenty years older, took on the task of bringing up young Pip. She was married to Joe Gargery, a strong, kind man with fair, curly hair and blue eyes. Joe was a blacksmith in the village, which lay on the flat and marshy Thames estuary, not too far from the sea.

JOE GARGERY

Joe was big and strong, but he was a little frightened of his wife. Pip was frightened of her too. Mrs. Joe—that's what everyone called her—was quick to fight with both Pip and Joe. She fought with words, and sometimes even with a cane.

Though Pip couldn't remember his parents, sometimes he went to the churchyard and gazed at their gravestones.

Pip was in the churchyard one Christmas Eve. The day was growing

darker and he shivered as the wind rushed in from the river. He was feeling sorry for himself and began to cry.

"Hold your noise!" cried a terrible voice.

A huge man sprang up from among the gravestones. He was dressed in ragged gray clothes. He was wet and muddy, and shivering. Worst of all, he had an iron chain locking his ankles together.

"What's your name, boy?"

"Pip, sir."

"Where do you live?"

His hand trembling, the boy pointed to his village about a mile off.

"Where's your mother and father?" growled the man.

"There," said Pip, nodding toward the tombstones. "I live with my sister, Mrs. Joe. She's married to Joe Gargery, the blacksmith."

"Blacksmith, eh?" said the man, looking at the chain around his ankles. He stretched out his large hands and squeezed Pip hard by the cheeks. "Here's what you're going to do, boy. Go home and bring me back some food and a file tomorrow morning. If you don't —I might just eat you instead, starting with these fat cheeks of yours."

Pip ran home in terror. His sister was on the rampage and started shouting at him. She stamped her foot, shook her fist and screeched questions about what mischief he had been up to.

Later, during tea, Pip managed to hide a slice of bread and butter for the gray man on the marshes. In the distance, they heard the booming sound of a cannon being fired. Joe said it came from the

prison ship moored in the estuary.
It meant that a prisoner, a convict,
had escaped.

Pip hardly slept that night. Very
early on Christmas morning, he
crept downstairs and took some
cheese, a little brandy in a bottle,
and a beautiful round pork pie from
his sister's pantry.

He ran through the misty morning until he found the gray man. Seizing the food and drink, the man gulped it down like a starving dog.

Pip plucked up the courage to say, "I am glad you enjoyed it."

In reply, the man made a strange clicking sound in his throat. He demanded the file taken from Joe's workshop, then seemed to forget about the boy. When Pip left, the man was filing away furiously at the chain around his legs.

Mrs. Joe had guests for Christmas dinner. One of them was Mr. Pumblechook, Joe's uncle, who had a mouth like a fish. He and the other grownups lectured Pip about how grateful he should be to his sister for bringing him up.

Worse followed when Mrs. Joe went to fetch the pork pie from the pantry. Pip knew the pork pie had been swallowed almost in one gulp by the man on the marshes. At any moment his sister would return empty-handed and on the rampage.

Pip thought it best not to be there when this happened. He broke away from the dinner table and ran to the

front door ... straight into a group
of soldiers.

One of them, a sergeant, was
holding a pair of handcuffs.
Thankfully, they were not looking for
a pork-pie thief, but for the escaped
convict from the prison ship.

Everyone was excited at the prospect of hunting down a fugitive. Only kind-hearted Joe whispered to Pip that he hoped the prisoner would not be found. Pip hoped so too.

Joe and Pip set off with the soldiers and a handful of people from the village. It was cold and dreary, and Joe carried the boy on his back over banks and across ditches. There was a sudden cry of alarm to their right. It didn't come from the soldiers. They headed toward the sound.

A man was floundering in a patch of swampy ground, about to be sucked under. It was dark now, but even without seeing him clearly Pip knew that it was the man in gray. Three soldiers dragged him from the muddy bog.

When they had brought him out,
he was so covered in slime that
you could not tell the difference
between the mud and the rags he
wore. He looked up and saw Pip,
who shook his head slightly. The
boy didn't want the mud-covered
man to think that he'd led the
soldiers to him.

"We've got you now, Abel Magwitch," said the sergeant.

"I want to say something, in case anyone else gets the blame," said the prisoner. "I broke into a blacksmith's close by. I stole a file and a pork pie."

"You are welcome to the pork pie," said Joe. "Whatever you've done, we wouldn't have you starve to death."

The convict said nothing, but again came that strange clicking sound from his throat. It was as if no one had ever said a kind word to him before.

The sergeant and the soldiers led him away.

"What will happen to him, Joe?" Pip whispered.

"It'll be back to the prison ship for Mr. Magwitch," said Joe. "And then he'll be taken to Australia."

"Australia? Where's that?"

"Not sure, Pip. A long way off, though."

Pip fell asleep as Joe carried him home on his back.

SATIS HOUSE

Pip never really thought about what he was going to do in his life. The reason he never thought about it was because he already knew. He was going to be a blacksmith like Joe. Pip had already started helping Joe in the smithy.

Things quickly changed when Mr. Pumblechook announced that Pip had been invited to meet a rich lady. She lived in the market town nearby. Her name was Miss Havisham and she wanted a little

boy to go and play at her grand
house.

Mrs. Joe said this was a fine thing.
Mr. Pumblechook said this was a
fine thing. No one asked Pip what he
thought. He was washed and scrubbed
and dressed up in his smartest
clothes. Then Mr. Pumblechook
drove him in his carriage to Miss
Havisham's house. It had a strange
name: Satis House. Through a fence
of iron bars Pip could see a courtyard.
All the windows on the ground floor
had iron bars on, too.

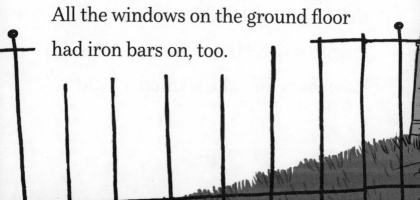

Mr. Pumblechook rang a bell by the gate. After a while, a young girl strolled across the courtyard holding a bunch of keys. She let Pip in, but told Mr. Pumblechook he wasn't wanted by Miss Havisham. At this

news, Mr. Pumblechook's mouth looked more fish-like than ever.

The girl said almost nothing, apart from telling Pip to hurry up. She called him 'boy', even though they were about the same age. But she was so beautiful and confident that she seemed much, much older.

Inside the house, it was dark. The girl picked up a burning candle and they weaved their way through a maze of passages until they came to a door.

"Go in," she said.

"After you, miss."

"Don't be ridiculous, boy. I am not going in."

Half afraid, Pip knocked on the door and was told to enter.

The room was large and well-lit with candles. Heavy curtains covered the windows. In an armchair sat the strangest lady Pip had ever seen. A white veil dangled from her white hair. She was dressed all in white. Jewels sparkled on her neck and hands.

"You are the boy sent by Pumblechook?"

"Yes, ma'am. I am Pip."

"Come closer," she demanded.

As he drew near, Pip saw that her long white dress was faded and yellow with age.

"How old are you, Pip?"

"Eight, ma'am."

"I have not seen the light of the sun since you were born, Pip."

Since Pip didn't know what to say, he said nothing. Then Miss Havisham told him to summon 'Estella'. Very uncertain, Pip went to the door and called "Estella!" into the dark corridor. He was pleased to see the beautiful young girl arrive back, holding her candle.

Miss Havisham wanted to watch Estella and Pip play cards together. The only game he knew was a simple one called Beggar My Neighbor. Estella beat him at several games. She didn't smile once in all the time they played. She made rude remarks about Pip's clumsy hands.

Finally, Pip was allowed to go home, but told to come back again in a few days. Estella almost pushed him out of the iron front gate and then locked it firmly. Pip was pleased to leave, but sad, too. It was nice to have someone to play with.

Back home, Mrs. Joe and Mr. Pumblechook peppered Pip with questions about Miss Havisham and Satis House. Pip made up a story about how Miss Havisham was tall and sat on a velvet couch. From the way Mr. Pumblechook nodded in agreement, it was obvious he'd never been inside Satis House. Pip felt a little guilty about telling lies in front of Joe.

A Mysterious Benefactor

This was the start of many visits to Miss Havisham's. Pip didn't enjoy them, though he was always glad to see Estella. And Estella was always glad to be rude to him. She often remarked on how 'common and coarse' he was.

Pip found out that Miss Havisham had adopted Estella, and she liked to watch them play together.

There were sometimes other visitors to Satis House. These were distant members of Miss Havisham's family. Once, Pip got into a fight with a tall, pale boy. He didn't start it, but he won. Estella was secretly watching, and she allowed Pip to kiss her afterward. It never happened again; the fight or the kiss.

Pip's visits went on for several years, until the time came for him to learn Joe's trade as a blacksmith. The apprenticeship was drawn up properly and legally in front of a magistrate in the nearby market town. It meant that the young man's time with Miss Havisham—and Estella—was at an end.

Estella was moving to London to become a lady. Meanwhile, Pip was going to stay in the village and become a blacksmith, just like Joe. Once, Pip would have loved nothing better than to be like Joe:

an honest skillful worker. But his regular visits to the grand house had made him want more than that. He had no choice, though. What else could he do?

In front of him stretched a life of working in the heat and sweat of the blacksmith's forge. There was more work to be done at home now, too. Mrs. Joe had been seriously injured. Now she sat quiet, tame, and incapable in a corner. No more rampaging. A girl from the village called Biddy came to help Pip and Joe look after her.

Then, one day, something happened to change everything.

By now, Pip was in the habit of going to the village pub, The Three Jolly Bargemen. One Saturday night, he and Joe were there with some others when a strange man came in. He watched them from his seat and kept biting his finger as if it were a tasty snack. Then he stuck out that finger like an accusation.

"I believe," he said, "there is a blacksmith by the name of Joe Gargery among you."

"That's me," said Joe.

"You have an apprentice known as Pip?"

"That is I," said Pip.

The stranger didn't recognize Pip, but Pip remembered him. He had passed him once on the stairs at Miss Havisham's, a long time ago. He had a large head and bushy eyebrows. Pip had thought he must be a member of Miss Havisham's family.

But no. It turned out that he was a lawyer from London. His name was Jaggers, and he wanted to speak to Joe and Pip privately. The best place to do this was in their parlor at home. It was hardly ever used after Mrs. Joe's accident.

Mr. Jaggers sat down at their parlor table and said, "Mr. Pip, you have a benefactor. Do you understand what that means?"

Joe's and Pip's blank faces showed that they did not.

"A benefactor," went on Mr. Jaggers in his deep voice, "is a person who wants to do something good for you, and who has the means to do it. That is to say, the person in question has money. Your benefactor, Mr. Pip, has great expectations for you and wishes you to go to London."

"Why?" said Pip, shocked. "What am I going to do in London?"

"You will learn how to be a gentleman, and gentlemen do not have to do anything."

"Who is this kind benefactor?" Pip asked, though he already knew.

It had to be Miss Havisham! She wanted him to become a gentleman so that he could marry Estella!

"I cannot say." Mr. Jaggers replied. "Your benefactor wants to remain unknown until the day he—or she—chooses to reveal their identity."

There was plenty more to listen to and be amazed by. Meanwhile, Joe hardly said a word.

OFF TO LONDON

Within a week, Pip said his goodbyes to Joe, Mrs. Joe, Biddy and Mr. Pumblechook. Now that he was starting on the road to becoming a gentleman, they behaved differently

toward him. It was almost as if he were a stranger.

That morning, carrying a little suitcase and quite alone, Pip caught the coach to London.

First Pip called at Mr. Jaggers' office. The lawyer was Pip's guardian. He would provide a monthly allowance of money until Pip's benefactor chose to appear.

"Welcome, Mr. Pip," said the lawyer. "What do you think of London?"

"It is very big," Pip said, "and—and busier and dirtier than I expected."

Pip hesitated to say this because he thought it might be rude. Mr. Jaggers simply laughed. He explained that Pip was to live with a young gentleman called Herbert Pocket. He would be taught about books and manners by Herbert's father, Mr. Matthew Pocket. The Pockets were all distant cousins to Miss Havisham.

When Herbert and Pip met, they gazed at each other in surprise. He was grown up now of course,

but Herbert was the same tall,
pale boy Pip had fought at Miss
Havisham's. But Herbert didn't
bear Pip any grudge. In fact, he
was very friendly.

Herbert explained the reason why Miss Havisham stayed indoors and always wore the same old white dress. He said that years ago she was supposed to marry a man. But on the morning of the wedding, he wrote to her breaking off the marriage.

"Did you ever notice the clock in her room?" said Herbert.

"Yes, it was stopped at twenty to nine," said Pip.

"That is the time she received the letter. Everything froze in time at that moment. The dress she wears is her wedding dress."

Herbert said that Miss Havisham had trained Estella to be cold and to treat people, especially men, as cruelly as Miss Havisham herself had been treated. Estella was trained to break men's hearts.

Joe came to visit Pip at his lodgings in London. Pip introduced him to Herbert, who was very gracious. But Pip was embarrassed by Joe, even though the village blacksmith had dressed in his Sunday best. Joe even called him 'Sir' when he always used to say 'Pip'.

Sometimes Pip saw Estella, too. She had grown into a beautiful lady. She was no longer rude to him. The two were almost friends, though she never returned his smiles.

Pip believed that his benefactor was Miss Havisham. If she wanted him to become a gentleman, she must have changed her mind about wanting Estella to break men's hearts. Maybe Estella wouldn't break Pip's heart, at least.

Pip went back to his old village a few times, including for the funeral when his sister, Mrs. Joe, died. But he no longer belonged there.

Things went on like this for some years. In London, Pip learned to dress better, to behave better, to speak French, and to ride a horse. Everything a gentleman should do.

He often spent more money than he should. Mr. Jaggers, who provided his allowance, would wag his bitten finger and tell him to stop spending so much. Then Pip would ask him when the identity of his

benefactor would be revealed. He already knew who she was
of course.

"You'll know in good time, Mr. Pip," was all Mr. Jaggers would say.

The time finally came.

A SURPRISE VISITOR

It was a dark and stormy night. Herbert, with whom Pip still shared lodgings, was away. Their rooms were at the top of an old house near the river. The wind shook the windows and blew the smoke from the fireplace back down the chimney.

Suddenly, Pip heard the stumble of a footstep downstairs. He took the lamp and went out onto the landing. The stairway lights had blown out.

"Which floor do you want?" Pip called.

"The top," said a deep voice.

The man climbed up the stairs. He wore a rough coat. Long. iron-gray hair flowed from beneath his hat.

"What do you want?" said Pip.

"You, Mr. Pip. I wish to come in."

From the look on the man's face as the lamplight fell across it, he seemed pleased to see Pip. But Pip did not know him.

Once inside, the man shrugged off his coat and stood near the fire. The way he held his large brown hands out to the heat suddenly made Pip realize who he was.

The man saw the recognition on Pip's face.

"Yes, it's me! Abel Magwitch. From the prison ship. The man on the marshes that you helped by bringing food and a file to when you was a lad."

Pip stepped back in horror.

"Weren't you taken to Australia?" he gasped.

Many prisoners, men and women, were transported by boat to serve prison time on the other side of the world, in Australia. There they could eventually be

freed, but they would never be allowed to return to England.

Magwitch told Pip that he'd served time for his crimes. Once free, he had done well and made money as a sheep-farmer in Australia. Lots of money.

"If I'm caught back in England, I'm done for," said Magwitch. "But it was worth it to see what a fine gentleman my boy has become. Look, you're wearing better clothes than me. And is that a gold ring on your finger, my boy?"

Pip nodded. He had a terrible suspicion what was coming next.

"Who paid for them clothes and ring, Mr. Pip?"

"It was you!" exclaimed Pip. "You are my benefactor."

"That's the lawyer's word which Jaggers uses. I'd rather say I'm a friend to you, Mr. Pip. I'm like your second father. You helped me once. And I've been helping you ever since."

That night Magwitch slept in Herbert's room. Pip couldn't sleep at all. The rain and wind drummed heavily against his windows.

He asked himself again and again: how could he have been so stupid?

Miss Havisham had never been Pip's benefactor. Yes, Mr. Jaggers was her lawyer, but he was also Magwitch's lawyer.

So Miss Havisham had never intended for Pip to marry Estella. Everything Pip had in his new life as a gentleman had come from a criminal. He felt ashamed.

These thoughts were chased away by the knowledge that Magwitch's life would be over if he were caught. He had risked not just his freedom but his life to see Pip.

Pip was in Magwitch's debt, and had to help him get to safety. He needed to get him out of the country before he was captured.

Herbert returned the next day and Pip spilled all these secrets to him. Good friend that he was, Herbert agreed to help in Magwitch's escape.

This was urgent, for Magwitch
believed that he might already have
been spotted on his return to London.

The only way was to get Magwitch
on board a steamboat, bound for
somewhere far away. Magwitch
could not risk boarding in London
itself. Instead they planned to row

downriver to a remote place on the Thames estuary. They would stay there overnight and catch a passing boat to Holland or Germany.

While they were planning, there was a tragedy. Satis House burnt to the ground and Miss Havisham died in the fire.

The place where Pip had first fallen in love with Estella was gone, taking with it any remaining hope that Estella would return that love. But Pip had no time to feel sorry for himself. He and Herbert had to get Abel Magwitch safely out of England.

Magwitch's Escape

Magwitch was the calmest of them all when they embarked on the first stage of the escape. Herbert and Pip pulled at the oars, but he sat smoking his pipe in the stern of the little

rowing boat as if they were on a
pleasure trip.

Pip was no longer frightened
of Magwitch or ashamed of the
connection between them. Abel
Magwitch had only tried to do
good by him, and now he would
do good by Abel Magwitch.

They stayed overnight at a
dingy public house called The
Ship, whose sign squeaked in
the wind. The next day was
bright and clear. They waited

at the entrance to a creek, watching for the smudge of smoke from the approaching steamboat.

There it was! As fast as they could, Herbert and Pip steered

the little boat out into the river.
They aimed to draw alongside the
steamboat, whose paddles beat
through the water. On the side it
said 'HAMBURG'. This steamboat
would take Abel Magwitch to
Germany.

At the same moment that they
reached the open river, a large

rowing boat filled with policemen pulled out from the riverbank. It steered toward them. The police's boat was faster.

Pip's boat continued frantically on its path and the police followed. Just as the three of them reached the steamboat, the police rammed them with their bow. Abel had been crouching in the stern.

Now he was thrown overboard. Pip was afraid that he had been struck by the steamboat's paddles and pushed under. But as the Hamburg steamer thudded by, he saw a body floating in the water.

The police dragged Abel out. He was still alive, but only just. Nevertheless, they put him in handcuffs.

Pip was allowed to go back with them in the police boat, while Herbert returned to the shore.

Abel Magwitch could barely speak. "You can leave me now, my boy," he said. His voice was so faint that Pip had to bend close to hear.

"Never," said Pip. "I will never leave you. I will be as true to you as you have been to me."

There came that strange clicking sound in his throat that Pip remembered from long ago.

Pip Returns to Satis House

There is no need to make a longer story of it. Abel Magwitch died in the prison hospital. Pip was with him until the end.

Abel never knew that his plan of making Pip into a gentleman had failed. All of

Magwitch's money was confiscated because he had broken the law by returning to England. Pip was left with nothing. But Abel Magwitch had changed Pip in other ways. Changed him for the better, perhaps.

Pip returned to the little village where he was brought up. There he

discovered that Joe and Biddy had married. He was glad for them.

After that, Pip went to Satis House. It was a ruin because of the fire. Only the bare stumps of walls and blackened floors remained.

There was a figure wandering in the ruins, just like him. It was

Estella, tall and elegant. Pip had only ever known her to be cold and emotionless. Now her sadness was clear in the way she moved.

Pip picked his way through the remains of Miss Havisham's old house.

"Estella," he said.

"Pip?" Estella said. "Is that you?"

"Yes. It's me."

"Good."

Though it was growing dark, Pip could see her clearly now.

She was smiling.

Charles Dickens

Charles Dickens was born in Portsmouth in 1812. Like many of the characters he wrote about, his family were poor and his childhood was difficult. As an adult, he became known around the world for his books. He is remembered as one of the most important writers of his time.

To download Charles Dickens activities, please visit
www.sweetcherrypublishing.com/resources